ANN MARGUERITA has written this second book for the children of our world, so that they may feel happy and safe as they travel through the stories and are taken into their own sweet dreams.

Fannie Annie
and her
Little White Shoes

Fannie Annie
and her
Little White Shoes

Ann Marguerita

ATHENA PRESS
LONDON

ISBN: 978 1 84748 259 4

First published 2008 by
ATHENA PRESS
Queen's House, 2 Holly Road
Twickenham TW1 4EG
United Kingdom

Printed for Athena Press

Holiday Time

Clickety, crunch, went the pretty white leather shoes, as Fannie Annie trod on as many tiny stones as she could find to squash, on the white pavements near her home. Playing hopscotch on her own was such fun, especially listening to the sound her leather shoes made as she hopped up and down onto the hard ground. It gave her such pleasure. She could walk forever, just looking down admiring her brand new shoes, with the little strap going across her foot and the pearly button to do it up with. How she loved to look nice! Her long dark-brown hair was plaited into long pigtails and fixed tightly on top of her head with plenty of hair grips and a pretty pale-blue satin bow, matching her layered frilly short gingham dress which was all pale-blue and white little squares. With her white socks and pretty shoes, she felt very special indeed.

'We are going on holiday today and I'm going on a train and a boat,' she called out to her friends, Harry and Johnny, who were across the busy main road.

'You lucky devil, wish we could come too,' they shouted back to her. She waved goodbye excitedly.

'All right, Fannie Annie, calm down, or you will make yourself unwell,' Auntie Kitty warned her, as she came out of the house with a packed suitcase. Fannie Annie laughed, her bright green eyes twinkled with delight as she jumped onto some more stones to

crunch as she ran to take hold of her dear auntie's hand.

'Off we go now to catch the bus which will take us to the railway station, then we will soon be on our way to the Isle of Wight.'

It was just the two of them: her brother Roger was a little too young to take as well, and Uncle Ted had to keep working. Fannie Annie's mum and dad could never afford such a holiday, so this was a great treat to go away for a whole week, especially to a strange place. It made her feel very grown up. It felt like such an adventure and she was so happy.

The train puffed into the station. There were a lot of people waiting to go on their holidays. One by one the big doors were flung open as everybody got off.

'Auntie, can we sit at the front by the engine?' asked Fannie Annie very nicely.

'Yes, all right, my cock sparrow, just mind how you climb those big steps into the carriage.' So up she went in her little white shoes, noticing a large gap between the steps and the platform and thinking to herself that such a big hole was very dangerous, being only a thin little girl of seven.

She was a bit anxious for a moment, about falling right through that space, just like she was constantly told that once she had her bath and the dirt was washed away, she would go down the plug hole. A great big shiver came all over her at the very thought of disappearing down the drain and she quickly told herself not to think about such things.

'Well, we are on our way, my cherub,' Auntie Kitty said, now feeling excited herself and looking forward to a nice rest.

'I can't wait, Auntie, oh look at all those horses and cows in the fields and look at all the lovely grass and flowers!'

Fannie Annie never got to see such sights, living by factories and main roads. Her nose was squashed right up against the window as the train sped along. She couldn't resist standing up and looking out, with Auntie Kitty tightly gripping her dress from behind, not trusting the train doors.

'*Puff, puff, whistle,*' went the train as it sped on its way mighty fast.

'Right, in you come now, because we are going to go through a tunnel,' Auntie Kitty said. Then they were in real darkness, Fannie Annie didn't like that too much, she cuddled up to her auntie and felt safe.

Out of the tunnel they came, and when her face was back in daylight, Auntie Kitty burst out laughing. 'There! I told you not to look out of the window, now you are all covered in sooty smuts from the smoke, you look like a chimney sweep!' She licked the corner of a hanky and cleaned Fannie Annie up, but thank goodness her little white shoes were still spotless.

'Time for something to eat. What would you like, egg sandwich or cheese?' asked Auntie Kitty.

'Cheese please, Auntie.' Then they both had a nice cup of tea from the Thermos flask; it felt just like a picnic!

'I believe we are nearly at our station,' Auntie Kitty told Fannie Annie.

'Then we are going to get on a big ship, aren't we, Auntie?' asked Fannie Annie, wondering how big it would be. Her dad, being a Royal Marine, had shown her pictures of his ship and that was mighty big. Fannie Annie felt very small. She wanted to hurry up and get much taller.

They had to catch a bus from the train station which took them right in to the port. Their ship was waiting to take them across the sea to the Isle of Wight, a tiny little island where holiday makers loved to go.

'*Hoot, hoot*,' came from the ships large funnel; it was telling people to hurry up and get on board for the journey. There were lots of children with their mums and dads, which made Fannie Annie remember her own mum who wasn't very well, and then she felt sad, but the noise of the children laughing with excitement cheered her up again. She hoped that some of the children might be going to her holiday camp, so that she could play with them.

Hello, Isle of Wight

'Are we nearly there, Auntie?' Fannie Annie asked. She had loved every moment on board the great big ship, but there were lots of people and it was very noisy. The sea looked very deep, with big waves lashing against the side of the ship. She wished her dad had taught her to swim, remembering the story that he had told her, about being thrown in to the deep end of the swimming pool when he joined the Royal Marines, because he couldn't swim. Right now, dry land would be very welcome indeed. The longing to get to the holiday camp was all she could think of.

'Not far to go, Fannie Annie! When we get off this ship, a lovely coach will be waiting for us, so you must be patient for a little longer,' Auntie Kitty told her.

'I can hardly wait, I'm so excited.' Fannie Annie grabbed her auntie's hand, giving her a great big kiss on her cheek, realising just how lucky she was to be having a holiday.

'I can see dry land!' Auntie Kitty pointed it out for Fannie Annie. 'Now be ready to get off pretty nifty, before all the crowds get going.'

The big ship docked very quickly, and before they knew it they were sitting on the coach, right at the very front, ready for the last leg of their journey. Fannie Annie started to yawn.

'It's been a lot of travelling for you,' Auntie Kitty

laughed. 'You will soon liven your ideas up once we get there and be off having lots of fun.'

'I'm looking forward to seeing where we will be staying, Auntie, and how soft my bed is,' she replied, yawning again.

On the coach everyone was happy and excited. People had started to sing along together, which encouraged Auntie Kitty to join in. Fannie Annie absolutely loved all the joy that surrounded her, as the voices bellowed out, *My old man said follow the van and don't dilly dally all the way*, which was such a catchy tune all the children started to pick up the words too. Even the coach driver joined in.

Around the corner you could see the cliffs and the ocean, the sun was shining brightly, all the beautiful villages they were passing struck Fannie Annie with awe: she had never seen so many pretty little thatched cottages. They all had so many lovely flowers in their gardens. There were little streams with ducks in them and tiny little shops. She wondered how it must feel to live somewhere so delightful.

'OK, folks, we are arriving at Bembridge now. If you look to your left, you will see Sandown holiday camp, so are you ready, campers, for a great holiday?' the nice coach driver asked them all.

'Oh yes,' they all answered back, loud and clear.

'I will be here to collect you all next week for your return journey. Have a lovely holiday!' he replied. The coach pulled in to a large gravel courtyard, right in front of the reception area, where they all had to pay for their holiday and collect the keys to the chalets where they would be sleeping for the week.

One by one they stepped off the coach, giving the driver a tip for being so kind and friendly.

'Thank you, Sir, Madam; let me help you down those big steps, little missy,' as he lifted Fannie Annie up in the air. 'My, you have got a nice white pair of shoes on!' he remarked.

She blushed and said, 'Auntie is going to teach me how to dance, and I'm going to wear my best shoes because they make a nice noise.'

'You are a lucky little girl, aren't you?' he laughed.

'Come on, tinker,' Auntie Kitty said, taking her hand, and in to the reception they went.

'Well, our chalet is number seventeen; let's go and find out where we are going to stay all week,' Auntie Kitty said to Fannie Annie.

So off they went, feeling the breeze from the ocean on their faces, and listening to the sound of the waves splashing against the seashore was such a joy to them both.

'Here we are at last,' Auntie Kitty said, as she put the suitcase down to unlock the door to the chalet. 'We are so lucky to be here on the side by the cliffs and the ocean.' Fannie Annie sat down on to her bed to test how comfortable it felt.

'I love my bed, it is so soft, but I can't wait to go out and start exploring!' In a great big hurry she started getting ready to go out and have fun.

'Change your clothes and those pretty shoes, save those for best eh?' Auntie Kitty suggested. 'First of all, I think it best that we both go and get our bearings together, I don't want you to get lost.'

'I won't get lost, Auntie, I promise,' she answered.

'You will be free to run around soon enough, when I know where everything is, cherub.'

'OK then,' Fannie Annie replied.

'Let's go and find the main hall and see when our meal times are, then you might see some children of your own age to have fun with,' Auntie Kitty suggested to her.

'Let's go now, Auntie!' cried Fannie Annie, as she started to pull her hand halfway out of the chalet door in her eagerness. They both explored the site thoroughly, discovering all sorts of places that Fannie Annie could go to quite safely, as the camp was only small; it was more like a large family experience.

'Look, there's the hall, that's where all the fun will be had, also the dancing that you are so looking forward to; this is where we will eat our meals as well. It's not far for us to go from our little chalet is it?' Auntie Kitty said, feeling pleased about everything.

'I love it here already,' Fannie Annie replied, then started to believe that she was dancing: round and round she swirled on her tip toes, until she made herself feel all giddy and fell onto the grass laughing, knowing she was going to have such fun here.

Happy Holiday Camp Days

In the big main hall lots of people were gathering for their evening meal, when all of a sudden over the loud speaker came a voice.

'Hello, campers, welcome to Sandown holiday camp, may we wish you all a very happy holiday.'

Then, one by one, they all went slowly in to the large dining hall, the smell of delicious food drifting in to the air, making them feel very hungry.

'This is our table, Fannie Annie, let's sit down and claim our seats, then we will sit here all week,' Auntie Kitty told her. Across the table sat a big chubby boy with very rosy cheeks. He gave a nice little smile to Fannie Annie, she gave a shy smile back, but as soon as the food started to be served, boy, did he like large portions! His chubby fingers kept grabbing whatever came along, and lots of it too; his mum and dad never told him off once.

'Please may I be excused, Auntie?' Fannie Annie asked, once she had finished her meal and was feeling full up.

'Off you go now and be good,' Auntie Kitty told her.

'I will,' she answered. As she got up to leave, the fat boy got up too. 'What's your name?' asked Fannie Annie.

'I'm Paul,' he answered.

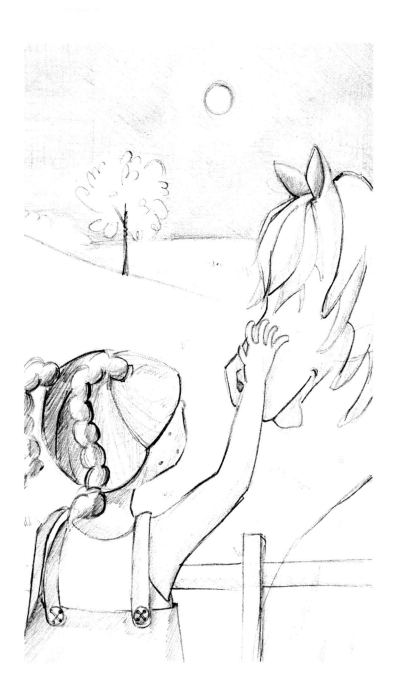

'Shall we go and see the horse in the field, Paul?'

'I would like that,' he replied. So they both ran to stroke the beautiful white horse, although poor Paul, being so chubby, had a bit of trouble trying to keep up with skinny Fannie Annie, who ran like a greyhound.

'My brother, Roger would like it here, Paul, but he is only two and a half and I'm seven, so my auntie brought me on holiday on my own,' Fannie Annie said, looking for a four leaf clover while she sat on the grass, enjoying her freedom.

'Do you want to stroke the horse then?' Paul asked her.

'I'm going to,' she said, bravely getting up very quickly to show that she wasn't afraid, although the horse was certainly big. She slowly put her hand up, and he allowed her to touch his head very gently.

My, he has got such big sad eyes, Fannie Annie thought, *and he is so gentle; he is pure white just like my shoes.* 'I would like a horse of my own, wouldn't you, Paul, but he would have to live in a lovely field just like this. Stroke him, he won't hurt you,' she told him.

Paul went close to the horse and looked up at how big he was, but backed away nervously saying, 'He might bite me, just look at his big teeth!'

'No he won't, silly,' she giggled.

More children came running over to see the horse. They gave him some titbits from the dinner table to eat and they patted him without any fear.

'I like this horse,' Fannie Annie said, trying to make some new friends.

'We've been here longer than you so he knows us better,' a little boy replied. 'Anyway, do you and your friend want to play chopsticks with us in the hall? We also know a great den where nobody will ever find us.' It all felt very exciting to Fannie Annie and Paul.

'Cor, yes we will play with you,' they both nodded. They all ran off together laughing, except Paul who followed at a slower pace, with his chubby, freckled face getting very red and hot.

The other children were two boys called Dennis and Bertie and a little girl called Mary.

'Shall we show you our den then? Follow me,' said Bertie, being cautious and not wanting any adults to see where they were all going, because he liked it being a secret. 'This way,' Bertie ordered them all. 'Duck your heads because we are going underneath the big hall and it is dark and cobwebby in there so be careful.'

They all squeezed through a tiny gap, except Paul had a bit of a struggle pushing himself through, so Fannie Annie and Dennis grabbed Paul's clothes and pulled him through.

'Thanks, you two,' puffed Paul, pleased to have made it in with the help of his new friends, and hoping there might be a larger hole along the way to get out of.

'Do you believe in goblins?' said Dennis, mischievously.

Fannie Annie answered back quickly, saying, 'Don't know about them, but I'm sure there are pixies and fairies out there, especially when it's dark.'

'Nah, don't be stupid,' Bertie scoffed, although he did seem a bit scared at the thought. 'Anyway, how do you know for sure?' he questioned.

'Well, sometimes I think they speak to me and tickle

me when I'm going to sleep,' Fanny Annie said quietly, remembering all the pretty pictures in her books and felt for sure she was right.

'I know there are goblins too, because they chase me in my garden, making funny noises and laughing at me, but only when it's dark and I'm on my own,' Dennis said.

'What do goblins look like?' asked Mary, feeling nervous about this conversation and where it was going

'They are like elves, but they are naughty and can do bad things,' Dennis told her.

'Don't worry, Mary,' said Fannie Annie, holding her hand to comfort her, 'because the fairies and the pixies will always look after you, especially if you are good, and they will chase those naughty goblins away, so there,' she answered, poking her tongue out at Dennis.

'You lot are talking rubbish,' Bertie piped up. But it was awfully dark where they were, so they decided to go back outside and play in the hall.

Mary had some brightly coloured chopsticks; there were a lot of them, they looked like slim knitting needles but plastic. They all sat on the floor and started to learn to play.

'You hold them up in the air, then drop them,' Mary instructed them all, 'then you have to try and pick one up at a time without moving any of the others.'

Fannie Annie loved this game, but the boys got fed up with it.

'We will see you later.' Bertie said. 'Come on, let's go and explore some more.'

'Are you coming dancing tonight?' asked Fannie Annie.

'Blooming hope not; we want to be tough,' they laughed. 'We expect we will have to though,' they moaned, knowing how much their mums and dads liked to dance and have a goodnight sing-song before bed. 'Anyway, it's great staying up so late on holiday.' That brought a great big grin to all of their faces.

'See you later, alligator,' Dennis sung out,

'In a while, crocodile!' laughed Fannie Annie.

Beach, Cliffs and Poppy Fields

'Good morning, campers; are you bright and breezy and ready for some fun? Before the games start, come and have a hearty breakfast in the dining hall!' blared the great loud speaker; it gave Fannie Annie the giggles.

'Auntie, we had better hurry up or we will be late for breakfast and *you know who* might eat it all!' So out of the chalet door they both went, laughing merrily, joining all the other campers on their way.

'Morning, my dear,' said a nice elderly gentleman to Auntie Kitty.

'Good morning,' she replied politely. 'It's going to be another beautiful day, perfect for a lovely walk or a paddle in the sea,' she said to him, and he nodded in agreement.

Fannie Annie had run ahead to meet her friends and to catch Paul going in to breakfast, because this morning she really fancied a freshly cooked bread roll with her scrambled egg and baked beans and knowing Paul, and how he loved bread rolls, she was desperate to claim one before he ate them all. His mum and dad never told him not to be greedy; Auntie Kitty's blood would boil when he started to shovel all the food he could manage into his mouth, while everybody else ate normally.

Oh well, thought Fannie Annie, *perhaps he is always starving*.

'Let's have a nice stroll along the cliffs today,' suggested Auntie Kitty to Fannie Annie. 'The sun is shining brightly and it is so lovely and warm,' she said joyfully. 'It feels wonderful to be close to the sea!'

So off they went, down the hill from the holiday camp to the cliffs. There was a low white fence all along the edge, which overlooked the sea and soft sands below. Boats could be seen in the distance, although they looked quite hazy through the heat of the day.

'Auntie, can we go down to the beach this afternoon?' Fannie Annie asked longingly. She could hardly wait to splash in the water and play on the sand.

'Of course we can, there are fun and games going to be played by our holiday camp later anyway, we might as well go and watch, but be prepared for a lot of steps to climb down and then back up,' Auntie Kitty warned her.

'That will be good; I like steps,' – nothing bothered Fannie Annie, it was all a wonderful adventure to her.

'Auntie, this is the best time that I have ever had,' Fannie Annie said, looking up and smiling at her, as they walked together arm in arm. They could feel the warmth of the sun on their faces, with the sea breeze blowing through their hair, the seagulls singing above their heads and to top it all the millions of beautiful poppies they could see all around them, as far as the eye could travel, swaying from side to side.

'If I didn't know any better I would think that this was heaven,' Auntie Kitty laughed with sheer joy.

'Auntie, what is heaven?' asked innocent Fannie Annie.

'Well, cherub, it is the most beautiful place in the world, where the angels live; there are no more sad things to worry about and nobody gets sick any more,' she replied.

'That sounds like a nice place, Auntie, it's where Jesus lives isn't it?' said Fannie Annie, remembering what she had learnt at Sunday school.

Looking up to the blue sky and feeling the greatness of this experience, she knew that life was very precious and special. 'I'm going to thank Jesus for my holiday and ask if he will make my mum feel better when I say my prayers tonight,' she said, quietly nodding her head.

Auntie Kitty knew she had a sensitive little soul and she loved her dearly. 'That will be lovely, Fannie Annie,' Auntie Kitty answered, giving her a kiss.

They both walked through the poppy fields until they couldn't walk any further, feeling totally refreshed and suntanned. All Auntie Kitty's freckles had started to show. Fannie Annie was getting an all over healthy glow, with her little sundress and sun hat on. They arrived back at their holiday camp just in time for lunch.

'Mary, Dennis, Bertie!' Fannie Annie shouted to her new friends, as she ran to talk to them on their way to lunch.

'Where have you been all morning?' asked Bertie, inquisitively.

'We've been on a long walk along the cliffs. Are you all coming down on the beach after lunch?' Fannie Annie enquired, hoping that they were.

'Expect we will, knowing my Mum and Dad, they

will want a paddle. Dad loves to go in for the competitions as well, so I am going to take my beach ball, then we can all have a good game, what do you say?' Bertie asked her.

'Yes, not half, I like playing ball, then we can look for coloured stones and pretty seashells as well,' she suggested.

'You can, cause us boys will look for crabs,' Bertie laughed, 'then we will chase you and Mary with them!' How he loved to torment the girls!

'Well we will hide, won't we Mary, and you will never ever find us, so there.' Fannie Annie always gave as good as she got; she tried hard not to show fear, even if she was petrified of crabs.

Lunch was soon over, all the campers were excited and looking forward to some fun on the beach. Fannie Annie and Auntie Kitty were soon on their way down the many steps, with bucket and spade, towels and sun cream.

'Mind yourself on these steps; they are very old and tiny,' Auntie Kitty warned Fannie Annie.

'We are nearly down now, Auntie, I can see the sea, and hear the waves, it looks lovely,' she answered, pulling her sandals off quickly as her feet touched the silver sand, making her quiver with delight. Then off she ran heading straight for the sea, feeling the soft, warm sand run through her toes.

'Fannie Annie, don't you want your bucket and spade?' Auntie Kitty called out to her.

'No thanks, Auntie, I'm going to have a paddle and splash in the sea,' she called back. Luckily her

FINISH

swimming costume was a very bright yellow, so Auntie Kitty would be able to keep her eye on her quite easily. Anyhow, she fancied a nice paddle herself.

The games started, with an almighty cheer from all the campers.

'Right, are we ready for a three-legged race?' shouted Ricky, the very handsome man in charge of the games. Fannie Annie heard him, even though she was enjoying her splash in the sea. She decided it was time to have some fun of a different nature.

'Auntie, I want to play these games,' she said excitedly.

'Well, you had better find yourself a partner,' she advised her.

'Bertie, Bertie, will you be my partner for the three-legged race?' Fannie Annie shouted out to him, as he was busy building a great big sandcastle with a moat all around it.

'OK,' he laughed, 'Just make sure that we win, eh!' as they both ran to join all the other children.

Once they had tied a bright blue scarf around both of their legs, with a struggle, they were ready to run the race as best as they could. Lots of children were laughing and falling over with the giggles, as they found it very difficult to stand still, with one leg tied up to another.

'Right, everybody, GET READY, GET SET, GO!' shouted Ricky the holiday camp manager. The children started running and falling over, as one partner always wanted to go faster than the other. Luckily, the sandy beach cushioned the children's falls. Fannie Annie and Bertie were doing quite well, they seemed to be getting the hang of it.

'Don't pull my trunks so tightly, Fannie Annie,' Bertie told her.

'Well I can't help it can I, cause you are nearly pulling my swimming costume off, silly,' she said crossly. Whoops! Over they both fell.

'Get up, Fannie Annie!' Bertie shouted, 'Cause we are going to win, hurry up, because the others are catching us up!' They both managed to get themselves up onto their feet again and made it to the winning post.

'Yippee!' shouted Bertie, waving his hands up in the air, listening to the applause from all the adults.

'We came first, Auntie!' called Fannie Annie, running over to tell her, so pleased with herself and Bertie.

'Well done, my little cherub, now you and Bertie may well receive a prize at the end of the holiday.'

'Goody! Goody! Goody!' she yelled out with pleasure.

Next came a sack race for the adults and plenty more to follow, although Fannie Annie, Bertie, Dennis, Mary and Paul preferred to play hide and seek. Running free, laughing out loud at all the little tricks that they played on one another, they had a wonderful time. Bertie managed to catch some crabs with Dennis and Paul; they kept them in seawater in their buckets, and then tipped them around their sand castles in to their moats, that they tried so hard to keep filled with water, but the sand kept soaking it all up.

Fannie Annie and Mary found the most beautiful sea shells that they had ever seen: they were all pearly with lots of pretty colours on.

'I'm going to keep these shells for ever,' Fannie Annie said to Mary.

'Yes, me too, I'm going to show my teacher,' Mary answered. 'I had better find some more, because my mum will like them and my Nan, and I bet my friends will want to play swoppies with them for beads.'

'Oh, yes!' Mary replied. So off they busily went looking very carefully along the water's edge, not wanting to miss a single sea shell.

Dancing Feet

'Let's go, Fannie Annie, have you got your dancing shoes on?' laughed Auntie Kitty.

'I'm really looking forward to learning to dance,' Fannie Annie answered, doing a twirl in her pretty, flared, white dress. It had tiny lilac flowers all over it, and what with the dress and her long dark hair, the little white shoes stood out perfectly, and matched the big white satin bow in her hair. There was no doubt she looked a picture.

'My, you will be the belle of the ball, you look just like a fairy princess! You might meet your handsome prince tonight,' Auntie Kitty said jollily.

'Not likely, Auntie, I'm not that keen on boys,' Fannie Annie quickly replied in no uncertain terms.

'Wait until you are older, my girl, you will soon change your tune,' she was told.

'No way, Auntie!' she laughed out loud, although there was a very nice, shy boy at school called Jeffery Gordon. She had caught him once when they were playing kiss chase in the playground; she remembered it because she had run straight into a brick wall afterwards and given herself a bad nose bleed.

I didn't like Jeffrey Gordon anyway, she thought to herself. How glad she was to be at the dance with her new set of friends, especially as there were some nice boys. Although, Fannie Annie would never admit that

she liked boys to her Auntie Kitty. That would be too embarrassing for her!

Quickly changing the subject, Fannie Annie said nervously, 'Look at all the people here, don't they look posh, Auntie? My friends are all here too,' hardly believing such a change in how everybody looked. Mary was dressed very prettily, in a pale-pink chiffon frilly frock with her long, blonde, curly hair pulled back with a huge pink bow. The boys were a bit sheepish trying to hide behind their mums and dads, acting as if they really didn't want to be there at all.

The band started playing a slow tune and the dance floor got busy straight away with people longing to dance. The first tune was a waltz.

'Right, Fannie Annie, are you ready to learn this dance?'

'Yes, Auntie, I hope that I can learn it,' Fannie Annie said, as she jumped up quickly, raring to go.

'Right! One, two, three; one, two, three,' Auntie Kitty told her, as she started to guide Fannie Annie across the dance floor. Fannie Annie was watching her little white shoes at all times, trying her hardest to dance nicely; then, when she was really getting the hang of it, Bertie caught her eye as she looked up, and to her horror, he was blowing raspberries at her and laughing out loud. His dad soon stopped all that, by getting hold of him by the scruff of his neck and telling him off for being so rude.

'Take no notice of him; boys are silly sometimes,' Auntie Kitty told her.

'Oh, I don't care, cause I'll chase him tomorrow and pinch him, hard,' said a defiant Fannie Annie.

'Now, now, my girl,' smiled Auntie Kitty, trying hard not to laugh too much.

It was a wonderful evening, with lots of dancing; the music was so happy, and there was even a sing-song to all the old songs gone by, like *Roll out the barrel, lets have a barrel of fun*. Fannie Annie kept pretending that she could tap dance, because the little white shoes made a lovely sound on the wooden ballroom floor; she was skidding in them as well, when Auntie Kitty wasn't looking.

'I like your shoes, Fannie Annie,' remarked Mary, 'I wish my Mum would buy me some just like yours, then maybe I could dance like you,' she said enviously, looking down at her plain little sandals.

'Ask your mum nicely, Mary, then I'm sure that she will. I will let you try them on if you want,' Fannie Annie said, now feeling sorry for her friend. Mary's face lit up with happiness at the very thought. So, the two girls sat down together to swap shoes. Luckily their feet were nearly the same size. Mary started to do a little dance, copying just what Fannie Annie had been doing.

'What are you up to, Mary?' her mum said, looking down at her daughter's feet. 'Oh I see, you want some nice shoes just like your friend. Well all right, I'll see what I can do; I'll have a word with your dad later.' Mary took the little white shoes off and returned them to Fannie Annie, feeling extremely grateful for the dancing she was able to do in them, and thought Fannie Annie was very kind.

As the evening came to an end, one by one, the people slowly left the big ballroom, some still singing.

Once outside, how dark it felt to Fannie Annie! She put her arm in Auntie Kitty's, then they called out, 'Goodnight, sleep tight,' to all the friends that they had made while on holiday.

'What are they, Auntie?' Fannie Annie shrieked, as some small flying creatures seemed to be dive-bombing them as they walked back to their chalet to go to bed.

'Nothing to worry about, cock sparrow, they are just bats and they come out at night. What a beautiful clear night it is, just look at all those stars twinkling so brightly in the sky, and just listen to the sound of the waves; it's a bright and breezy night,' Auntie Kitty said to Fannie Annie, taking her mind off feeling frightened about the bats.

They were soon back to their cosy chalet and dressed in warm pyjamas in no time at all.

'Right, time to get into bed now! My, how you will sleep well tonight,' Auntie Kitty said smiling, giving her a goodnight kiss and tucking Fannie Annie in tightly, saying, 'We don't want any more falling out of bed, do we now?' A few times she had fallen out onto the floor in her sleep.

'Auntie, will the wind blow our chalet off the cliffs, while we are asleep?' Fannie Annie asked, wide eyed.

'My girl, what will you think of next, no of course not, silly billy! Say your prayers then off you go to sleep. Sweet dreams, night, night, sleepy head,' said a weary Auntie Kitty, yawning, as she climbed in to bed herself, ready for a well-deserved rest.

Fancy Dress and Prizes

'Oh, what a beautiful morning, oh what a beautiful day, I've got a beautiful feeling every things going my way,' Auntie Kitty was singing merrily, when Fannie Annie opened her eyes after a lovely sleep. She was surprised to see her busily making something out of some pretty coloured paper.

'Auntie, what are you doing?' she asked interested, leaping quickly out of bed so as not to miss anything.

'Well, this is for you to wear in the fancy dress competition today, you are going to be Queen Elizabeth.'

Fannie Annie was thrilled to bits, 'It's lovely, aren't you clever, Auntie, and I've even got a crown! I wish I could do something like that,' she said, wondering how on earth you could sew paper together so well, to make such a pretty dress. 'How much longer have we got on our holiday, Auntie?' asked Fannie Annie, bouncing around on her bed. She could never sit still for very long – Uncle Ted would say to her that she had ants in her pants, it's just that so much energy was bursting out all over her and she couldn't help herself.

'We still have two more days to enjoy ourselves, then I'm afraid it's back to the grime and the nitty-gritty side of life,' Auntie Kitty answered.

'What's "nitty-gritty"?' asked a puzzled Fannie Annie.

'Well, it means dusty old roads, factories and hard work, so that I can save some more money for another whole year, so that we can come on holiday again,' she replied.

'I will go to work too, and help you to save up for another holiday. I'm good at sweeping and shopping and I can sew a little bit, I'll work harder with my Mum as well, to take her on a nice holiday just like this one,' said a very determined little girl.

'We can plan that for next year then, cherub, then we will have all that to look forward to,' replied Auntie Kitty.

'There! Your dress is all finished, let's go and see what's going on before all the fancy dress competitions start. I tell you what, how about we go and buy some nice gifts to take back home with us for Mum, Dad, Roger, Uncle Ted and Great-Grandmother Large, that will make them happy. Come here, tinker,' Auntie Kitty took Fannie Annie's hand and off they went to the camp shop.

They bought a beautiful cat brooch for Great-Grandmother Large, sun hats for Uncle Ted and Fannie Annie's dad, a cute little singing toy bird in a pretty bright red cage for her mum, and for her brother Roger a bright blue toy car. Auntie Kitty paid for the gifts, the shop assistant had wrapped them all up in such nice crepe paper.

'They are lovely presents, Auntie, now I am going to look forward to giving them to everyone, it will be just like Christmas!' Fannie Annie skipped on merrily, to get ready for the fancy dress.

'OK, step very carefully into this paper dress,'

Auntie Kitty said. Fannie Annie did as she was told, because she sensed that it would tear otherwise. 'That looks really pretty! Now let's put on your crown.' She fixed it tightly, onto her head with plenty of clips, hoping that it would not fall off. 'Now you have to hold this, it's a stick that I've wrapped with paper and fixed with a round ball on top, the Queen had to hold something like this when she was crowned at her coronation, it was called a sceptre.'

'That's a very funny word, Auntie,' Fannie Annie said, looking strangely at the odd stick that she had in her hand.

'My, you do look good, even if I say so myself,' Auntie Kitty said, standing back admiring all her hard work.

'Right, off we go! You must walk slowly so as not to spoil your costume,' Auntie Kitty warned. With her little white shoes peeking out from under her dress, Fannie Annie felt so special, just like a fairy princess; she had never ever felt so different. As she walked very carefully over to the hall, lots of people were shouting out, 'Hello, Queen Elizabeth your Majesty! Hello, your Royal Highness!' They were bowing and curtseying, it made Fannie Annie blush and Auntie Kitty laugh.

Lots of boys and girls were going in for the fancy dress competition; there were soldiers, policemen, firemen, nurses and film stars. Bertie was Robin Hood, he looked great with his bow and arrow; Paul had been made into a big ball, all you could see was a little face; Mary was Little Bo Peep, and Dennis was dressed up as Dennis the Menace. That made Fannie Annie laugh out loud, because he had a big shaggy wig on his head, and his mum had put loads of freckles all over his face; it was just like the comic that she loved to read every week. He gave Fannie Annie a big scowl because he was feeling very silly: lots of grown ups were getting the giggles too. Lots of children were hoping to win the fancy dress competition; music started to play in the large hall, then a loud voice came over the microphone from Ricky the holiday camp manager.

'Right, children, I want you all to walk slowly around the hall so that we can all have a good look at the wonderful costumes you are wearing, a great big well done for all the hard work put in by the parents.'

Everybody clapped loudly and cheered, as the children paraded around the hall, with beaming smiles. Fannie Annie's crown fell off once, and poor Paul tripped in his roly poly costume and couldn't get up again – a nice man had to put him back on to his feet. Dennis the Menace never stopped scowling, because folks kept pointing at him in fits of laughter, and Bertie just showed off, holding his bow and arrow, making out he was ready to fire. He aimed it a few times at Fannie Annie and Mary but they just gave out a squeal and giggled.

The time came soon enough for the winner to be chosen: the children made a nice straight line and hoped that they would be chosen, but alas it could only be one of them.

Ricky stood and clapped loudly for all of the children, 'OK mums and dads I need your help here, the loudest claps will be the winner.' That's what they did: one child after another received claps, but the

loudest claps of all went to Dennis the Menace. The children were all very good sports, they knew they would all receive a nice gift just for taking part in the contest, besides there would also be prizes for all the sports activities that had taken place down on the beach.

One by one they started to go up onto the stage.
'Well done, Fannie Annie, for being such a good sport in the three-legged race, and you too, Bertie,' he congratulated them both.

'Now these presents are for your wonderful fancy dress costumes, I do hope that we will see you both here again next year,' he said to them. They both nodded their heads enthusiastically.

It took quite a while to give out so many presents, but all you could hear was the sound of ripping paper and screams of delight at the wonderful toys the children had received.

'Look what I've got, Auntie!' Fannie Annie was thrilled with her gifts, she held them out to show Auntie Kitty.

'What a lucky girl you are,' Auntie Kitty said.

One present was a pretty pink vanity case, in which she could carry all her special things around, it had a comb and mirror in the lid as well. The other gift was a toy white horse, with a little brown leather saddle and reins on its back, she really loved this present, because it would remind her of the real horse for ever and ever, so she put him safely inside the vanity case, ready to take back home.

'Mary, what are your presents?' asked an inquisitive Fannie Annie.

'I've got a very pretty necklace, and a lovely baby doll,' Mary answered. 'They are really nice, aren't they?' she said to her friend.

'I just wish we could all stay here for ever, don't you, Mary?' they both looked at each other very sadly. 'We will have to swap addresses before we go, and I want you to write in my autograph book too,' Fanny Annie said. 'Let's go and find the boys and see what their presents are, shall we?' The two ran off together calling, 'Bertie, Paul, Dennis, where are you?'

The boys were in a corner of the big hall, racing cars back and forth to each other. Bertie had a toy plane and bright red racing car, Paul had a big bouncy ball and a fire engine and Dennis had a toy water pistol and a police car.

'We think our presents are the best!' Bertie shouted, 'I just wish we didn't have to go home, because this holiday has been the best time that I have ever had,'

'Yes,' agreed Paul. Dennis scowled again at the thought of going home, which made them all laugh and just for a moment they forgot the holiday was almost over.

Goodbye, Campers!

Fannie Annie and Auntie Kitty were up bright and early for the last day of their holiday. The suitcase was almost packed for their homeward journey, just the clothes left out for the day and to travel home in.

'Auntie, please don't pack my little white shoes, because I want to do a dance in them tonight with my best dress on,' said Fannie Annie, seriously. She wanted to make a lasting impression on all of her good friends.

'That's all right, cheeky,' replied Auntie Kitty. 'Look, here are your rough and tumble clothes for running around in, because I expect you will want to go playing hide and seek in all of your secret dens,' she laughed. 'We must have a nice paddle on the beach as well, and have a last look at the poppies blowing in the breeze along the cliffs. How very lucky we have been with such beautiful hot weather! My, there is a lot to do on our last day.'

Breakfast was soon over. Fannie Annie noticed that Paul seemed to be less greedy over his food now. Maybe he was fed up with getting so hot and out of breath when running around with the others and realised that he had been eating too much and it was slowing him down. Also, it can't have helped, getting stuck in that hole in the den. It was nice to see him being more considerate at the table.

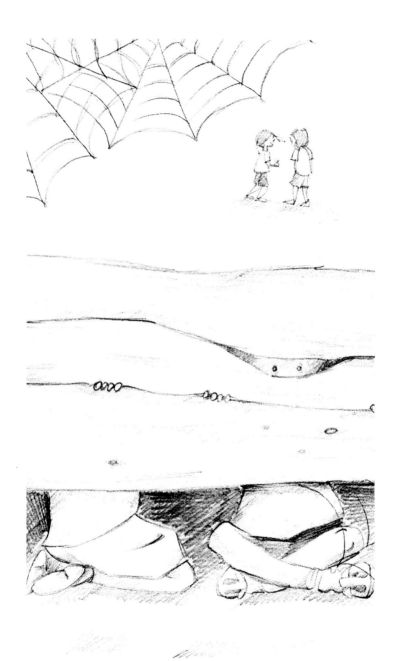

Bertie, Dennis and Paul waited for Mary and Fannie Annie outside the dining hall, so that they could play games.

'Right, who wants to play hide and seek in the den?' asked Bertie. They all put their hands up. The den was mighty big and dark underneath the holiday camp; they had discovered many tiny places that they could squeeze through, so off they ran, laughing and chatting.

'Paul, you go in that hole first,' suggested Bertie, who was more or less their leader; he knew that particular hole was the biggest. One by one they scrabbled through the hole after Paul, into the dark, cool space. They had made a table out of old bits of wood that had been left there, and all knelt down around it to talk to each other.

'Let's make a vow, never ever to tell anyone else about our den.' They all solemnly repeated the pledge out loud. Then they jumped up, laughing.

'Let's play hide and seek,' shouted Dennis. 'Us boys will hide together and then you two girls can hide together,'

'Yippee!' shouted Bertie. Paul wasn't so sure, as it was very dark, he thought they may get lost and never find their way out.

'Right, Mary,' Fannie Annie took her friend's hand tightly, 'We will hide first,' she said.

'Good, because we will soon find you both,' laughed Bertie.

'This way, Mary, follow me,' Fannie Annie whispered. The two of them, crawled under their little wooden table. 'Don't make a sound, Mary!'

'Hope you're ready; we are coming to find you!' Bertie called out. The boys made a right old din looking here, there and everywhere.

'Where are you girls?' called out Paul; he had started to worry in case they were lost.

'OK, we give up! You are too clever,' shouted out Dennis.

'Come on, Mary,' Fannie Annie crawled out from underneath the table first, to show her face.

'That was crafty, we never thought to look under the table, I didn't think you could get under that tiny space,' said Bertie. 'Our turn now girls, count to fifty, then come and find us,' Bertie instructed them both.

'Fifty!' the two girls shouted out a short time later. 'Ready or not, here we come.'

'This way, Mary, let's hold hands, it feels safer,' Fannie Annie started to pull Mary after her, looking in every corner; the two girls were not sure where to look next. All of a sudden, there was an almighty crash, making them jump out of their skins with fright.

'Bertie, Dennis, Paul, we give up now, are you all right? What was that loud crash?' Fannie Annie shouted, frightened. 'If you don't come out now, we are going to go for help.'

Then all of a sudden the boys called out, 'Over here, girls.'
Through the darkness, Mary and Fannie Annie saw three little faces. As they crept closer, they saw that the boys had found some planks of wood and stood them up against the wall, where they had hidden behind them. The crash was poor Paul managing to knock one over, giving the game away. Thank goodness everyone was OK; both girls gave a big sigh of relief.

'Let's go and see our white horse now,' Bertie suggested. 'Goodbye secret den! See you again another day,' they all sang out to their hiding place, as they squeezed through the gap to daylight.

It was lovely to feel the warm sun on their faces. They ran free as the wind, down the slope to the green fields near the cliff's edge, passing Auntie Kitty on the way to see their beautiful white horse that was contentedly grazing.

'Don't forget it's nearly lunch time,' she called out, remembering how good it felt to be a child herself.

'I know, Auntie, then can we go down to the sea to paddle, and can I bring my friends too?' she called out, stopping for a moment to see what the answer would be.

'If their mums and dads don't mind,' Auntie Kitty called back. 'Thank you, Auntie!' said Fannie Annie.

Lunch was as delicious as ever, but the children were in a hurry to get to the beach. They had gone straight to their chalets after lunch, to put on their swimming costumes and grab their buckets and spades. Most of the parents decided to join Auntie Kitty down on the beach. Down the narrow little wooden steps they went, there must have been about one hundred and thirty altogether, it certainly was a long way down, but worth it when you finally got there.

'How I love the soft sand, it tickles my toes,' Fannie Annie said with glee.

'Come on, gang, follow me,' called Bertie. The children were quite happy to do just that, because they were all truly good friends. Bertie's mum and dad laughed, saying, 'He's not a bad boy, he just likes to be a leader and look after everyone.'

The parents sat on the sand and had a good chat, then they went for a paddle. How warm the ocean was! Auntie Kitty and the mums held their dresses up above their knees as the waves splashed against their legs, and the dads rolled up their trouser legs. They were really enjoying themselves. Hearing the laughter of the children playing nearly brought a tear to Auntie Kitty's eyes, for she knew that this holiday had been something very special for them both and they would remember it for ever.

As they all climbed back up the tiny wooden steps to the cliffs above, the first thing to greet them all was the bright red poppies blowing in the breeze. There were so many of them. Bertie ran through them, and then the other children followed.

'What a wonderful sight!'

'Isn't it,' they all agreed.

'Let's take some photo's to keep!'

Auntie Kitty took two very special photos, one of the children playing and another of the poppies with the sea in the background.

'Time to have a little rest and then get ready for dinner,' suggested Paul's dad. 'Then we can all meet in the hall for a good sing-song and dance tonight.'

'Bye for now, see you later,' they shouted out to each other as they went on their way to get ready.

★

'That was a lovely snooze we both had,' said Auntie Kitty.

'Yes, now I can stay up really late, can't I,' Fannie Annie said, really pleased. She had all her long hair wrapped in rags, so that it would be very curly; Auntie Kitty had wrapped them around lots of sections of hair, which made her look like she had sausages hanging all around her face.

'I'm glad you kept my prettiest dress out of the suit-case, Auntie, because it's my favourite colour, lavender,' said Fannie Annie, admiring it. After a nice bath and smelling all clean and fresh, she put her dress on, then Auntie Kitty started to undo her hair-rags, making lots of long ringlets. She fixed a white satin bow on the side.

'Where are my little white shoes, Auntie?' Fannie Annie asked as she started to search for them.

'Under your bed, silly,' laughed Auntie Kitty.

'I just love my shoes, I hope my feet don't grow too big, because I want these shoes to last forever,' Fannie Annie said, bending down and doing up her pearly button on the side, then doing a hop and a skip to remind herself of the sound that they make. She wriggled with delight at the sound.

'You are a nitwit, aren't you,' laughed Auntie Kitty. 'Come on, tinkerbell, let's go and have our dinner, it will soon be dancing time,' she said. Fannie Annie felt really loved when she was called these special little names. So off they went in their very best clothes all ready for the evening.

Their dinner was lovely: soup to start, with delicious hot bread, followed by roast chicken, roast potatoes, carrots and peas, then strawberry trifle to follow.

'My, Auntie, my tummy is full to the top!' Fannie Annie said, showing her just how big it felt.

'Well, cherub, you will soon burn all that food off with dancing and all the running round you are bound to do later,' Auntie Kitty said, giving her a little tickle, which gave her the giggles even though she was so full.

'Can I go to see the band in the hall now, Auntie?'

'OK, be good then,' came the answer.

'Paul, are you coming with me to see the band,' she asked nicely, across the table. Paul nodded, getting up from the table after asking to be excused. The two of them went rushing in to the large dance hall to hear the band playing very loudly. There were lots of people already gathering around, and some had started dancing.

'That's a very fast dance, I wish I could learn that one,' Fannie Annie said admiringly.

Across the hall were Bertie and Dennis with their parents, so they ran over to see them.

'Oh, there's Mary as well! You do look nice,' she said to her friend. Mary had the most beautiful dress on that she had ever seen: it was blue velvet tied with a pretty bow behind her back, and she was wearing a lovely pair of new shoes that her dad had bought her, they were white with a silver buckle on top. 'Mary, you can make crunchy noises just like me now,' she laughed, giving her friend a big hug.

Auntie Kitty had arrived, with Paul's mum and dad.

'Time for dancing,' said Paul's dad, as he grabbed his wife for a foxtrot, and all the other parents followed.

'Can we do this dance, Auntie?' asked Fannie Annie desperately.

'Come on then, we can do our best, or why don't you and Mary have a little shuffle around? Look, there are other children who are trying,' Auntie Kitty suggested, but Fannie Annie preferred her Auntie to try and show her the real moves because she wanted to feel grown up. She did learn a few little steps, and whirled around, from a waltz to quick step. She thought her little white shoes had something to do with how clever she felt, gliding around the dance floor, as if she were floating on air – it was such a wonderful feeling!

'Right, cherub, time to finish dancing, the sing-song is going to start now, so let's go and have a nice hot cup of Horlicks and a sing-song with our friends, before we go off to bed.'

Bertie, Paul and Dennis were tired and fed up with all the dancing, so they had kept themselves occupied playing with their cars. Mary had been learning to dance with her mum and dad too; she joined Fannie Annie and they went over together to see their friends who were crawling all over the floor, making loud engine noises, like *broom! broom!*

'Have you finished all that silly dancing?' laughed Bertie.

'It's not silly dancing, it's clever isn't, Mary, anyway we had a good time! Are you going to join in the sing-song?'

Right at that very moment the band started up, with Ricky the holiday camp manager, saying, 'Farewell and goodnight campers! Enjoy the sing-song and I hope to see you all again next year.'

Everybody gave a great big clap, and started singing.

> Goodnight, campers I'll see you in the morning,
> Goodnight, campers, I can see you yawning,
> Goodnight, campers, oh what a night, go and sleep tight,
> Goodnight, campers, goodnight.

That song was perfect to leave on; folks started to leave slowly, saying their goodbyes on the way out.

'I'll miss you all lots,' said Fannie Annie, to Bertie, Paul, Dennis and Mary. 'In the morning at breakfast will you sign my autograph book, please?' she asked.

'Yes, we will,' they all said.

'I will miss you too,' came from Bertie, 'except all that rubbish you talk about fairies,' he laughed. 'Nah, I don't mean it do I,' he gave her a friendly nudge and a cheeky wink.

Dennis said, 'I like you, Fannie Annie you are good fun, and I wish we never had to go back home.'

'Me too,' came from Paul. He gave her a big affectionate bear hug, which gave her the giggles.

'I will miss you very much,' little Mary said; she had never met anyone quite like Fannie Annie, she wished she could be her sister.

'Well, we can all write to each other, let's promise shall we?' So they all shook little fingers one at a time, which meant they would never ever forget their promise to each other, as long as they lived.

'Time for bed now, sleepy head, into bed you get,' Auntie Kitty said, as she tucked the blankets tightly around Fannie Annie, which always made her feel so nice and snug. 'See you in the morning, cherub,' as she gave her a goodnight kiss.

'Night, night, Auntie, I love you lots,' a little voice quietly whispered back. Then she said a prayer to herself that she had been taught at Sunday school.

'Jesu, keep me through the night,
That I may see the morning light,
And from my heart all evil take,
All this I ask for Jesu's sake. Amen.

'God bless Mum, Dad, Roger, Auntie, Uncle, Nanny and Granddad and Great-Grandmother Large.'

As she finished she was in dreamland, far away with the angels and fairies; her imagination ran havoc with her at times, but I guess that's what made her a little bit magic, and fun to be around.

Homeward Bound

Fannie Annie got all her friends to sign her autograph book, as they had promised, before each child was ushered away by their anxious parents so as not to miss the coach, which had just pulled up on the stony drive of the holiday camp.

'Morning, ladies and gentlemen, have you had a good holiday?' the nice coach driver asked them all.

'Beautiful mate, great,' came from the men; the ladies, replied, 'We've had a lovely time, the best time ever,' as they all started to board the coach, one by one.

'Well, hello little lady, and how was your holiday? I see you still have those little white shoes on, did you learn to dance in them?' he asked Fannie Annie.

'I can dance now, watch me,' she said, then she did a one-two-three with her feet, as if she was doing a waltz, round and round she went. 'My Auntie taught me that,' she told him.

'Well done,' he laughed, 'that was lovely, you are a clever girl; up the steps you go now, time to move on, little princess.'

It wasn't long before the coach was ready to go, loaded with lots of suitcases and folk, wishing they didn't have to go back home; it pulled out of the stony driveway onto the road, heading for the docks. Ricky, the holiday camp manager, waved them all off, wishing them a safe journey home.

'Now we are going back home, Auntie, I am looking forward to seeing Mum, Dad, Roger, Peter the dog, and my cat, Marmalade; I bet he's missed me stroking him,' Fannie Annie said in her dreamy-eyed way.

'Back in our own beds tonight, that's what I'm looking forward to,' answered Auntie Kitty.

The big ship had them across the water and into Portsmouth harbour, very quickly, and before they knew it, they were on the train travelling back home.

'We've had a lovely holiday, haven't we, Auntie,' Fannie Annie, said as she put her head on Auntie Kitty's lap. She was feeling very sleepy, and with the noise of the train, and her auntie stroking her head it didn't take long before she was in wonderland, fast asleep.

A loud screech made Fannie Annie wake up with a jump.

'Nothing to worry about, cherub,' said Auntie Kitty. 'The train is just coming to a halt, this is where we get off, so wakey, wakey, sleepy head!'

'Are we nearly home now?' asked Fannie Annie, yawning her head off.

'Yes, just a short bus ride and we will be back on our busy main road; it's a bit of a shock after the beautiful place we have just come from, isn't it? said Auntie Kitty.

Auntie Kitty lifted her suitcase, and helped Fannie Annie down the big steep steps of the steam train. The guard went along slamming the doors shut as the passengers stepped out, then he blew his whistle to let the train driver know that it was all right for him to move the train out of the station.

Fannie Annie waved goodbye to the train driver, saying to her Auntie, 'Trains are strong aren't they, a bit like an elephant.'

Auntie Kitty laughed, saying, 'What will you think of next?'

It felt good to be sitting on a big red bus, upstairs and right at the front, they had left their suitcase with the bus conductor below. As the bus travelled down the streets, it passed all the familiar places that they both knew.

'Look, Auntie, there's Georgina, she's in my class at school! We can see a long way sitting up here, I can nearly see where my Nanny and Granddad live,' Fannie Annie said pointing in the direction she thought to be right.

'I believe they do,' replied Auntie Kitty.

'Well, the next stop is ours, so let's make our way carefully down the stairs to collect our suitcase; hold onto the back of my belt so that you don't fall,' Auntie Kitty instructed her. The bus conductor helped them both off his bus.

'Thank you,' said a grateful Auntie Kitty.

The road was so busy and noisy, it made them feel a bit confused at first, and the dust and dirt seemed to be everywhere. What with the weather still being very warm, without the sea breeze it felt stifling to them both.

'There are our houses, Auntie, and look, there are my friends, Harry and Johnny! I'm back home now,' she shouted, waving.

'Hello!' they both shouted and waved back. 'Are you coming out to play later?' they asked as they ran up to see her.

Auntie Kitty, answered saying, 'She has to get in and change first boys, then we will see.'

'Okey, dokey,' they said.

No sooner had Auntie Kitty put her key in the door than Great-Grandmother Large was there, then Uncle Ted poked his head around the door.

'We are so glad you are home safe and sound,' they said. 'It's good to see you both looking so well and suntanned. Look at all those freckles!' laughed Uncle Ted

'Let's go and see Mum, Dad and Roger now, shall we?' Auntie Kitty said, searching through her bag for all the gifts that they had brought back from holiday.

'Here they are, Auntie,' Fannie Annie quickly gave Uncle Ted and Great-Grandmother Large their presents.

'Wow! I love my sun hat, this is very posh,' said Uncle Ted as he put it on, feeling very pleased with his present.

'You do look nice, Uncle,' she told him.

Then as Great-Grandmother Large undid her gift she said, 'My, oh my, this is the best brooch that I have ever seen,' and put it on herself straight away.

'I think it looks pretty on you,' Fannie Annie said, standing back and admiring her choice of brooch for her dear grandmother.

'You knew how much I loved cats, didn't you,' she laughed, 'I think Marmalade has missed you, you can take his food down to him tonight if you like.' Every night without fail Great-Grandmother fed the cats; she had one called Sandy and Marmalade was his brother.

'Come on, Auntie, I want to give Mum, Dad and Roger their presents.' So off they went, ten houses down the road to Fannie Annie's home. They went to the side entrance and Peter the dog was well pleased to see them both – his little tail nearly wagged off.

'Marmalade, Marmy, where are you?' called Fannie Annie. He came speeding through the garden like a rocket, not one bit afraid of Peter the dog, rubbing his body up and down Fannie Annie's legs and making her giggle, because it tickled so much.

'Mum, Dad, Roger, we're back!' she called.

'Oh, Fannie Annie, I've missed you so much,' her mum said giving her a great big hug.

'Me too, cheeky chops,' came a loud deep voice from the kitchen. Her dad came out and picked her up, lifting her right up into the air.

'Don't squash Marmalade's dinner, Dad,' she giggled.

A little face peeked out to see what all the fuss was in the backyard. 'Roger, I've got a nice present for you and Mum and Dad, here you all are,' said Fannie Annie, handing them all out.

'My, mine is big,' said her dad.

'And mine is a very strange shape, I wonder what it can be,' laughed her mum.'

'Mine, mine!' Little Roger's hand was eager to open his present.

'Wow! Look at my sun hat, it fits me perfectly,' said Fannie Annie's dad.

'Just look what I have got, a little bird in a cage and it sings, I love it,' said her mum.

'I got a car, *broom, broom*,' said Roger. He got the hang of pushing it straight away.

They all gave Fannie Annie and Auntie Kitty lots of kisses.

'Did you have a nice time?' asked Fannie Annie's mum.

'We had a very nice time,' said Auntie Kitty, 'lovely weather made it even better.

'I made some good friends who I played with, we had a den, and there was such a beautiful white horse there, Mum, I would love to have one if I was very rich,' said Fannie Annie, very wide eyed.

'We have certainly missed your cheekiness, and your being around to keep us on our toes and make us all laugh. Marmalade kept meowing while you were away, and Roger was lonely without you,' said her mum.

'I missed you all lots, but I said my prayers every night for you, and next year perhaps we can all go on a nice holiday together, that's right isn't it, Auntie, because we are going to work very hard to save lots of money to pay for it. I am going to do sweeping, polishing, shopping, and I will help you with your homework, Mum.'

Fannie Annie's mum always had lots of different squeaky toys to pack into boxes from a factory across the road – she enjoyed working from home.

'I can work very hard, I promise,' Fannie Annie meant every word.

Auntie Kitty gave her a great big cuddle and kiss, and said, 'Well, I'll be off now, I expect you will want to play outside with your friends, Harry and Johnny.'

'Thank you, Auntie for the best holiday ever, I really love you; and I love you lots and lots and lots Mum, Dad and Roger, forever, and ever, oh! and my Nanny and Granddad, Great-Grandmother Large, Uncle Ted, Marmalade and Peter the dog!'

'*Woof! Woof!*' he agreed.

'But we all love you the most, Fannie Annie,' said her mum, giving her a great big hug. 'Off you go then and have some fun,' laughed her dad. 'Don't forget to come back for tea, because we have your favourite cake.'

'Yippee! Jam doughnuts!' she shouted, as she ran merrily out to find her friends, and start more adventures.

Who knows what she will get up to next...

Printed in the United Kingdom
by Lightning Source UK Ltd.
128895UK00001B/26/P